Wild Rabbit

Field Hare

RABBIT SPRING

TILDE MICHELS

Illustrated by
KÄTHI BHEND

Translated by
J. ALISON JAMES

BULLSEYE BOOKS
ALFRED A. KNOPF
New York

DR. M. JERRY WEISS, Distinguished Service Professor of Communications at Jersey City State College, is the educational consultant for Bullseye Books. A past chair of the International Reading Association President's Advisory Committee on Intellectual Freedom, he travels frequently to give workshops on the use of trade books in schools.

Library of Congress Catalog Card Number: 87-18107
ISBN: 0-679-80153-7
RL: 2.8

First Bullseye edition: March 1990
Manufactured in the United States of America
2   3   4   5   6   7   8   9   10

Rabbit Spring

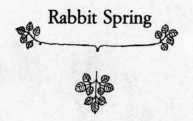

It was Rahm's nose that first appeared
out of the ground. He sniffed the morning
air. It smelled like grass and clover
blossoms.

"That's a good sign," said Rahm.
Climbing out of the hole, he pricked up
his ears and listened carefully. Mosquitoes
hummed and leaves rustled in the wind.
"That's good, too," he said.

Then, turning around, he called, "You can come out now, Silla. All's clear."

So Silla also climbed up out of the burrow. She sat up straight, sniffed, listened, and hopped over to Rahm. "I am absolutely famished," she said.

Both rabbits bounded into the open meadow. After five or six hops, they came to a stop and sat perfectly still. Then they looked around, cocking their ears in all directions. When they were sure no danger was afoot, they went on.

It was early morning. Although the sun was not yet up, the sky was already turning pale. Dew lay on the meadow, making the grass fresh and juicy. Silla stopped at a dandelion patch. Rahm began to graze a little farther away. Even while eating, they were fully aware of what was going on all around them. Crouched low in the grass, now and then they would break from chewing, cock their ears, and listen.

By the time the sun came up over the forest, they had eaten their fill. Side by side they hopped back to their rabbit burrow.

"I think it is time for us to build the nursery," Silla said.

At the last full moon, Rahm and Silla had mated. This litter of children would be their first.

"When do you think it will happen?" asked Rahm.

"When the moon is round again," she answered.

Rabbits don't count with days and months. They don't say "in May" or "in August." They say "when the clover is in flower," "when the corn turns gold," or "when the cabbage heads are full."

So Silla said, "When the moon is round again." And she added, "I want it to be a great big beautiful nursery."

"How many children do you think we'll have?" asked Rahm.

"There is no way of telling," she answered. "There could be four; there could be ten."

"Ten!" cried Rahm. "Isn't that a bit much all at one time?"

"Not necessarily," Silla answered. "A cousin of mine just had ten children, and my mother had more children than she could count. Eleven babies at a time were nothing for her. Surely that doesn't surprise you."

"I know all about these things, of course. But it still seems like a lot to me."

"Let's just wait and see," said Silla, and she slipped into their hole. Rahm followed.

The hole that Rahm and Silla disappeared into led to their rabbit burrow, an underground house that branched out and had several entrances. Many rabbits had added on to the house. They had dug tunnels and built chambers.

Nothing could be seen from above, except for the lookout holes.

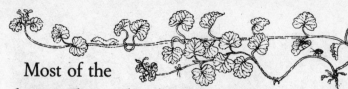

Most of the
burrow lay under the meadow, but
one section stretched out under the
forest. It was possible to go into
a hole in the grass and come out in
the woods.

Since rabbits are always having more
children, the burrow was
constantly being expanded.
Presently, there was enough room
in the den for ten families.

Rabbits like to live together in a
large group. Everyone helps to
care for the young ones. They
clean their fur together, and when
the weather turns cold, they snuggle up to
keep warm.

"Well, then," asked Rahm, "where do
you want your nursery to be?"
Silla scooted along the underground

tunnel. Along both sides the holes were occupied. She sniffed the walls and prodded them with her nose. Finally she said, "This spot is just right."

So they set to work.

Since the burrow was set into a sandy bank, it was easy to dig out tunnels and rooms.

Rahm and Silla scratched a hole in the wall with their front feet. With their hind feet, they shot out the loose sand. Then they pushed it backward along the tunnel.

Silla was happy that Rahm was helping her. Most buck rabbits leave the digging to the does, but Rahm was different. "Why should you do all this work alone?" he'd say. "You have to dig the hole, build the nest, and after all that, you have to have the babies!"

When the hole for the nursery was the right size, Silla said, "That's enough. It's just fine."

She bustled around a bit longer, smoothing down the walls. Then she started to pull wool out of her fur for padding the floor. "A nursery should be warm and soft," she explained.

Rahm admired the nest. He was very impressed with Silla's work.

"All this digging has made me tired," he said, "and I'm already hungry again. I think I'll go out to graze a little."

"Good idea," answered Silla. "Let's go get something to eat, then we can come back and take a nap."

She crawled from her hole into the tunnel, and they headed outside.

It happened precisely the way Silla said
it would. She gave birth to seven tiny
rabbits at the next full moon. Their eyes
were sealed shut—they could not see.
Their little ears were as round as mouse
ears—they could not hear. And they
didn't have a single hair on their
bodies.

After Silla had licked them clean, she called to Rahm. "Come take a look—we've got babies, and they are healthy and beautiful."

Rahm crouched next to Silla by the nest. Full of pride, he looked at his children and repeated, "They are healthy and beautiful!"

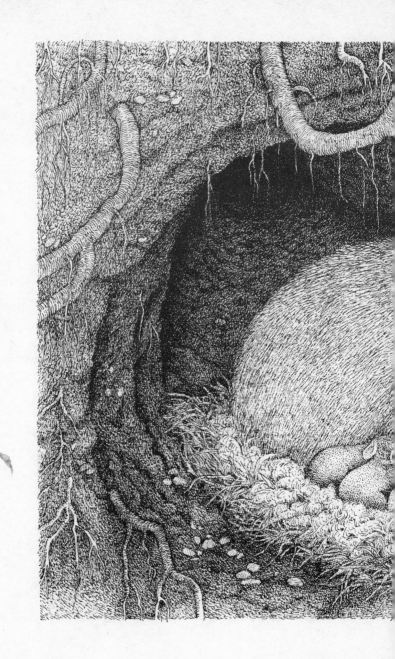

After that, Silla was constantly busy. She nursed the baby rabbits, and she washed them with her tongue.

She sat by the nest for hours watching them, crawling out of the nursery only when she was hungry. When she did, she stuffed the opening full of grass so that no one could disturb the babies while she was away.

Rahm slept with the other rabbits that night. The nursery was only for Silla and their young.

The following sunrise, Rahm went out to graze with the others. In the pale light of morning and in early evening, the meadow was full of rabbits. Sometimes there were as many as thirty or forty. The place was already hopping by the time he emerged.

Rahm was quite fond of his cousin Polko. He hopped over to him, and the two of them grazed side by side.

"Are you alone today?" asked Polko.

Rahm chewed up another peppermint blade before answering. "Silla had her babies yesterday."

"Your first litter?" asked Polko.

"Our first," said Rahm.

"How many did you have?"

"Seven. Seven healthy, beautiful babies."

"Seven!" said Polko. "That's not bad . . . for a start." He sat up and looked around. "By the way," Polko continued, "the field hares also have new babies."

Rahm shook his head so that his ears flopped. "Humph. Hares."

"What do you have against hares?"

"Humph," Rahm said again. "They aren't very sociable. Not one hare has ever said a word to me. They think they're better than we are."

"You're just imagining that," said Polko. "They're not very talkative, that's for sure. But you simply have to be the one to start a conversation. We speak the same language, you know. And we *are* related."

"Related," said Rahm. "They don't act like relatives. If we were related, we'd be hares, just like them."

"Well, in fact, we are hares," said Polko. "We just live a little differently."

"Much better," said Rahm. "Our life is much better. Just think of our burrow! It keeps us warm and cozy and safe."

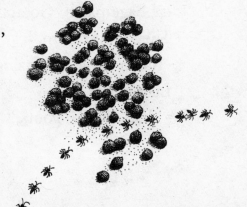

"I can't argue with that," said Polko. "Our den is a cozy place. The hares don't have a burrow under the ground—they don't have a proper home at all. Instead, they live in furrows or under bushes, places like that. I wouldn't like to be a hare."

Polko scratched himself, groomed his ears, and said, "Despite all that, they do have pretty children. Very pretty."

"They couldn't be prettier than mine," said Rahm.

"I'm not so sure about that," Polko answered. "I saw two of them, back there by the cabbage patch. Go and see for yourself. They're just born."

Rahm stopped grazing. "Just born? Like mine?"

"Exactly like yours," said Polko.

Now, that was exciting.
Rahm had never seen
newborn field hares before.
He had no idea what hares did
with their children and couldn't wait to
find out.

Rahm left his cousin and hopped across
the wide meadow. Then he ran along a
row of cabbages at the edge of the patch.
Here and there he'd nibble a tasty leaf;
here and there he'd munch up a young
cabbage plant. Every once in a while he'd
sit up and look around.

It took quite a lot of traveling to reach
the end of the cabbage field. When he got
there, the little
hares were nowhere to be seen. Rahm
ran along the last row.

Then, so suddenly that he almost tripped
over himself, he was upon them—two
baby hares.

They simply lay in a hollow on the bare earth, for they didn't have a nest like his own children. And they were all alone. No father or mother was anywhere near them. Cuddled close to each other on the ground, they didn't stir. Their fur was gray-brown, like the soil.

Rahm couldn't believe what he saw: Although the hares were small, their eyes were already open. The hares were really very tiny, the size of his own newborns, but they already had beautiful long ears and were completely covered with fur.

How can they be this way? wondered Rahm. *Open eyes; proper, long ears; beautiful, thick pelts!*

He thought of his own children—blind, deaf, and naked!

Rahm was disturbed. There was something very wrong with this. Deep in

thought, he hopped away from the baby
hares. He went along the cabbage patch

and over the meadow. He ripped out a mouthful of clover, but it had no flavor. He nibbled on a dandelion leaf—it didn't taste good. After a while he slipped back into his hole.

He tiptoed into the nursery. His children lay next to each other by Silla's side, nursing. Their little rosy bodies moved very tentatively. He watched as they wiggled around helplessly, trying to find a new nipple. They did look healthy and satisfied.

But Rahm saw only that they were naked, that they had sealed eyes and round, mouselike ears.

Silla noticed right away that Rahm was not himself. "Is something the matter?" she asked.

"Oh, I was only thinking. . . ." Rahm couldn't tell her what was on his mind. He didn't want to offend Silla.

But Silla didn't give in. "So, what is it?"

Rahm's ears hung down. "It's just that . . .
well, you know . . . that is, I mean. . . .
There are two little baby hares back
behind the cabbage patch. They're exactly
the same age as ours." Rahm stopped
talking.

Silla was quiet, too.

She licked the babies clean. She
straightened their nest and covered them
with the wool. Then she turned to Rahm.

"So you've been to see the baby hares,"
she said.

"Umhmm," said Rahm.

"And you've seen that they are further
along than our children."

"Umhmm," said Rahm.

"And now you don't
like ours anymore."

Rahm couldn't answer that,
not even with an "umm."

"Are you aware," began Silla a
little later, "that everyone, everything,

is a little bit different? Rabbits grow up like this, hares grow up like that. That's the way it's supposed to be."

Rahm glanced around the nest. "They're supposed to be this way?" he asked. "You really mean that?"

"They'll grow; they'll change," said Silla. "You must have a little patience."

Very soon after the next sunrise, Rahm ran back to see the baby hares. He could tell from a distance that their mother was with them. This time the little ones weren't lying motionless in their hollow.

They were hopping and rolling around in the grass. Rahm couldn't help thinking that despite their size, they really were just like grown-up hares.

He approached cautiously. The hares poked up their ears and sniffed. Rabbits rarely came this way.

Rahm spoke up in a reassuring voice, "I won't hurt your young. I only wanted to talk with you."

"Talk?" asked the mother hare.

Rahm realized how odd he must sound. "You see," he said, "we have babies, too, just like yours."

"I see," said the hare.

"Seven, in fact," continued Rahm. "We have seven children. We usually have a lot. You only have two."

"That's not true," said the hare. "I have four."

"Four? But I only see two."

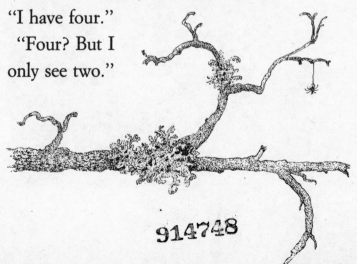

"That's right. Only two of them
are here. The other two are a
little ways away, in another
hollow."

"Why is that?" asked Rahm.

"Because it's safer. You know yourself
how dangerous the foxes and birds of
prey are. Two can stay hidden better than
four. If all four were hopping around
together, they would be easy to spot."

"And the other two," asked Rahm, "are
they all alone right now?"

"Of course," said the hare. "I can't
be in two places at one time."

"And the father?"
asked Rahm.

"Mother hares,"
said the hare,
"raise their
children alone."

Rahm was thoughtful. "With us," he said, "it's entirely different. Our babies live in a burrow under the ground."

And then he told her all about the soft, warm nest in the nursery and about the large extended rabbit family.

The two baby hares moved closer to listen.

When Rahm had gone away, they stormed their mother with questions. "Why don't we have a soft, warm nest?"

"You have a hollow and a soft, warm pelt that are just as good," answered their mother.

"And why don't we have a father?"

"No father!" said the hare. "What a ridiculous idea. Of course you have a father. He just doesn't live with us. The buck hares come around when it's time to mate, when it's time to have more young. And as far as I'm concerned, that is just

the way it ought to be. When you grow
up, you can try what you like and
decide what is right for you."

The two small hares were sisters and
looked almost identical. They could be

told apart only by their ears. Because one
had brownish ears and the other's were a
shade grayer, their mother named them
Brown-Ears and Gray-Ears.

"Tell us about the other two," begged
Brown-Ears. "Where are they?"

"They are on the edge of the forest,"
said her mother.

"Could we go there?" asked Gray-Ears.
"And what do we have anyway—sisters or
brothers?"

"One sister and one brother," said their
mother. "But the forest is still too
far away for you to go just yet.
Your legs have to get stronger,
so strong that you can run
away from the foxes and
hounds."

"Are foxes and hounds bad?" asked the
little hares.

"For us they are bad," explained their
mother. "Luckily, we are able to run
faster than they. It's not easy to catch
a hare."

"I want to learn how to run very, very
fast," said Brown-Ears. She sprang out
across the meadow. Gray-Ears followed
her.

"We'll go practice!" they both shouted
as they began
to hop
and to kick
their hind legs
into the air.

Then—suddenly (*what was that?*)—a
shadow fell across the grass.

It was not a great big shadow, not like a cloud. The shadow was small, and it flew over them.

"Duck down—fast!" called their mother.

The young hares pressed themselves flat to the ground. Covered with grass, they lay very still.

The mother hare had also leaped into a hiding place. With a pounding heart, she eyed the sky. There he was, the hawk. He circled directly over them, his sharp eyes searching the ground.

But he didn't spot the baby hares. After a while, he swung up high and flew away.

"That was well done," praised the mother hare. "If you had kept hopping around. . . ."

"What then?" asked Gray-Ears.

The hare pawed the ground nervously with her forefoot. "Then he would have discovered you, and he would have grabbed you away."

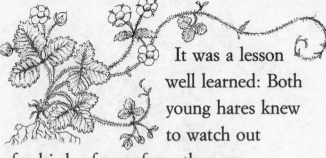

It was a lesson
well learned: Both
young hares knew
to watch out
for birds of prey from then on.

The sun, the moon, and rain-filled clouds
passed over the land.

The young hares grew bigger and
stronger. During the day, they lay in their
hollow and slept. At night and in the early
morning, they ran in the dim light across
the meadow. They practiced speed-racing,
and they began to graze on grass. They
still needed milk, but
their mother didn't
nurse them as often as
she once had.

One evening, the two little
hares were sitting in the grass with
ears cocked, waiting for their mother.

"Is she ever going to come?" asked
Brown-Ears.

"Where do you suppose she goes all the
time?" asked Gray-Ears.

"Maybe she's with our sister and
brother," said Brown-Ears.

"But it's not right that she should spend
more time with them than with us," said
Gray-Ears.

Finally, they saw their mother coming.
She wasn't hopping as usual. She was
running fast, faster than the young hares
had ever seen her run.

And a gigantic dog was right behind her.

With huge leaps their mother bounded
across the field. The dog was hard on her
tail.

"He's got her!" screamed Gray-Ears.

Then, as fast as lightning,
the hare turned in the
        air. . . .and ran in the other direction.

The dog tried to
turn, too, but was
running too fast. He
tripped over himself two
times. When he finally got to his feet
again, the hare had disappeared into the
thicket.

"Wow," whispered Brown-Ears.
"Our mother
sure tricked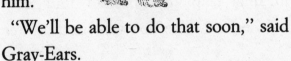
him."

"We'll be able to do that soon," said
Gray-Ears.

The huge hound sniffed around and ran

in circles where the hare had vanished,
but he couldn't get through the thick
undergrowth.

With a low growl, he slunk off.

As soon as the dog was safely away, the
hare ran over to her children, who curled
up to her and began to nurse straight
away.

The seven baby rabbits in the burrow were also growing bigger. As the season ripened, they developed great round eyes, thick woolly coats, and lovely long rabbit ears.

"Well," Silla asked Rahm, "what do you say now?"

Rahm looked at his children with pride. "They are just perfect, all seven of them. Now I understand."

That evening, the young rabbits were allowed to go out of the nursery for the first time. They crawled behind Silla through the underground tunnel into the open air.

Rahm had run out ahead. "Silla is coming with the children!" he called to his cousin Polko.

"I'm dying to see them," said Polko.

"You should be!" said Rahm.

"I'm sure you've never seen such perfect little rabbits. Just as I've been saying all along—you have to have a little patience."

Polko didn't answer, but his eyes twinkled with amusement.

When Silla appeared with her young, the whole meadow was full of rabbits. Almost all of them had come out of the burrow to graze in the dusk.

The world outside was new for the seven young ones. They romped and played in the grass. They tasted greens for the first time. And they investigated everything: peppermint leaves, fat bugs, even snails.

"You see," said Silla to Rahm, "I don't need to explain a thing to them. They understand it all without being told."

And Rahm said again, "They are

perfect, just as they ought to be!"

The sky turned a deep, dark blue.
Everything was still. The rabbits made
their way slowly across the grassy meadow
and grazed until they were full.

Every now and then they sat up straight
and cocked their ears, listening.

Suddenly, a sound broke into the quiet
of the evening—one that the little rabbits
had never heard before.

The oldest buck rabbit
was drumming. He thumped
the ground hard and fast with his
hind feet.

Instantly, the rabbits started running.
They ran to the burrow and dove into
their hiding places—leap and tuck, and
they were gone.

The meadow lay empty in the moonlight. Only the owl was there.

Silently, she appeared out of the dark branches and flew low over the earth. The little rabbits had escaped. But the owl had patience.

With her large eyes, she saw everything clearly, even at night. With her sharp ears, she heard the slightest stir.

There! She heard a rustling in the grass. Something scurried over the ground. . . .

The owl dove. A moment later she was flying again. In her claws she carried a mouse, which she took home to the three hungry owlets waiting in her nest.

In no time at all, the
young hares were making long
excursions. They had already
been to visit their brother and
sister on the edge of the woods.
Although they stayed together for the
most part, they learned to be alone and
to do everything for themselves.

When they were hungry, they ran to the
cabbage patch or the clover field. They
saw their mother less and less.

"Hey," said Gray-Ears one day, "have
you noticed that no milk is coming out of
our mother anymore? I think we're grown
up now."

Brown-Ears
began washing
herself. First,
she licked
her paw until
it was damp,

then she ran it over her face and head. Next came the ears, first the right, then the left. She pulled each ear down with her paw and painstakingly brushed it until it was smooth.

Finally, she licked her fur with her tongue and combed it through with her front teeth.

When she was finished, she answered Gray-Ears's question. "Of course we've grown up. Clover and cabbage leaves are my favorite foods now."

"What do you honestly think?" asked Gray-Ears. "Do the young rabbits have a better life? They live with their parents for a long time."

Brown-Ears had to think that over.

"Besides," Gray-Ears went on, "anytime a fox or an owl comes, they only have to slip down into their hole."

"You can't really say which of us has it better," Brown-Ears answered. "I like the way we are so free. And nobody has legs as strong as ours."

"That's true," said Gray-Ears. "No rabbit can run as fast as we can."

The two young does hopped over to the brook where the grass was juicy and tall—tall enough so that they could be invisible, even while they were eating.

Only their eyes and ears could be seen when they sat straight up.

"Look who's coming!" said Gray-Ears. It was their mother. But she was not alone. A buck hare followed her. "I wonder if that's our father."

But their mother was not acting very friendly. She kept a few hops away from

the male hare. When he tried to catch
hold of her, she leaped out of his reach.

He chased after her, and she had to run faster to escape him. Finally, the buck rushed at her with huge, springing jumps.

She turned on him and stood up on her hind legs. With her forepaws, she boxed him in the ears—*slap, clap*.

The strange buck turned and boxed back. But he was slightly smaller and weaker than the doe. He was no match for her.

He pulled back with his ears pressed flat against his head.

The little hares watched the fight with fascination.

"She doesn't like him," whispered Gray-Ears. "He couldn't be our father."

"Look how they've thrashed each other," said Brown-Ears.

"Our mother certainly is brave and strong," said Gray-Ears.

After that the buck skulked around and around their mother.

She paid absolutely no attention to him. Only when his paw came too close to her did she deal out a few blows. At last, he slunk away into the thicket.

Just then two more buck hares appeared at the top of the hill. They ran down the knoll, one from the left, one from the right.

When they got to the hollow, they glared at each other.

"Get lost!" said one.

"Who do you think you are?" asked the other. "You better hightail it out of here before I wallop you."

They both stood there stubbornly, glaring. Then, balancing on their hind legs, they struck out and began to box.

Smack, *whack* on the head.

Whack, *smack* on the ears.

Gray-Ears and Brown-Ears continued to peer over the tall grass.

"Why are they fighting?" asked Gray-Ears. "Do you know what's going on?"

"Maybe," said Brown-Ears. "Maybe they are both interested in our mother."

And that is just what it was. The buck hares were fighting over the doe.

But she acted as though it didn't concern her at all. She hopped around the meadow and grazed—ripping off a bit of clover, nibbling on a leaf of sage. From time to time she glanced over at the fight.

One buck was starting to look rather tattered. He was missing a piece of fur from his head, and his left ear was bleeding. After giving his opponent one last cuff, he decided he'd had enough. He turned around and ran away over the knoll.

The victor took a deep breath and shook his fur.

The doe looked over at him. And when he hopped over to her, she didn't run away.

"She likes that one," said Gray-Ears. "I think that is our father."

Brown-Ears said, "She's been waiting for that one. She's going to have babies again. I just know it."

"Because we're all grown up now," said Gray-Ears.

The two young hares didn't wait for
their mother after that day. They no
longer curled up together in their hollow.
Instead, they just slept wherever they
found a comfortable spot of ground.

Then one evening Brown-Ears said,
"Little sister, the time has come for
me to leave this place."

"Where are you going to go?"
asked Gray-Ears.

"Somewhere different. There are other
meadows and forests, you know. I'm sure
some of them are even prettier than this
one. And there are fields full of beets and
cabbage."

Gray-Ears was astounded. "How do you
know all that?"

"I've seen it from up there on the top of
the knoll. I'll be going quite soon. Would
you like to come along?"

"Not right now," said Gray-Ears. "I don't think I'm ready yet."

"Well, think about it," said Brown-Ears. "You can always change your mind."

She hopped over the grassland at a confident pace and soon disappeared behind a group of bushes on the knoll.

Gray-Ears stayed behind. *It doesn't matter*, she thought. *I'm grown up now. I can go where I want. Maybe I'll stay here, maybe not.*

She began to clean her ears, slowly and meticulously. Thin strips of mist drifted over the meadow. Then darkness laid itself down on the land. With it came noises, small voices. Gray-Ears listened. Frogs croaked in the marsh. An owl cooed. A moth brushed over the tips of the grass. Then, coming from the woods, she heard a rasping howl that silenced the other sounds.

She lifted her nose into the air to
catch a scent and stared at the edge of
the woods. Something dark moved

out of the thicket and came slinking nearer.

She sat up and took off with a bound.
Fleeing across the field, under bushes, and
over furrows, Gray-Ears knew instinctively
that she was running
for her life.

The fox was close on her tail. She
zigzagged, dodging through the grass, but
the fox kept following her. In a short
while, she was able to put a little distance
between them, and the distance gradually
grew.

Finally, Gray-Ears leaped through some
bracken and ducked into a hole under a
mound of earth. Her heart was racing
wildly from the chase. But she had won.

I've escaped, she thought to herself. *No
one can catch me; I can do anything, all on
my own—just like Brown-Ears!*

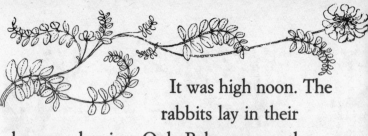

It was high noon. The rabbits lay in their burrow sleeping. Only Rahm was restless. Running from one hole to another he woke up rabbit after rabbit.

"Have you seen Polko?" he asked. "Polko is not in the burrow!"

Someone said, "He was grazing with us for a while in the twilight."

Another said, "We saw him in the early darkness, before night settled in. He was on the other side of the meadow, quite far away, actually."

Rahm was unable to find out anything more than that. "I'm worried about

Polko," he said to Silla. "Sometimes he just doesn't think."

"Do you think something has happened to him?" asked Silla.

Rahm didn't answer.

"Maybe a fox or an owl, or that huge dog?" she continued.

"Or . . ." Rahm hesitated.

"Or what?" Silla insisted.

"Oh, Silla, haven't you ever thought about it?"

"Thought about what?" Silla asked.

"About the terrible danger that none of us really understands," Rahm answered. "I don't mean a fox or any other ferocious animal. First there's a strange noise, a sudden sharp bang. And then one of us falls to the grass."

Silla began to shiver. "Rahm, please don't talk like that."

"Nobody wants to talk about it," objected Rahm. "But that doesn't change the way it is."

"And Polko?" asked Silla.

"I don't know."

The two of them curled up together with heavy hearts.

Everyone in the burrow was sad.

Mothers warned their children again and again, "Never stray too far from the hole. Beware of every shadow, every snapping branch. When the Oldest One pounds the ground, run like the wind to the burrow!"

Not long after Polko's disappearance, Silla complained to Rahm. "Our children have stopped listening to me."

"They are full-grown now, strong and clever. They don't need us anymore," said Rahm. "I think that they'll be leaving home soon."

"Leaving home?" cried Silla. "All seven?"

Rahm was silent. *Everything happens in its own time*, he thought. And he was right about that.

And so it was that the young rabbits grew wild and restless. Their nursery was stifling. There was no longer enough room for them all to live comfortably.

Rahm was right; the time had come.

"I'm going to find a hole of my own," said one of the young does.

"Me, too," agreed the first born. "I saw a spot in the burrow where we could easily dig out a couple of holes."

"Where?" two others wanted to know.

"Back where the main tunnel leads into the forest. The roof is nice and strong there. The tree roots make it sturdy." Four of the seven soon had made up their minds.

However, the other three didn't want to go along.

"Why should we have to stay in the burrow where we were born?" asked one. "I want to meet other rabbits."

"Perhaps we might even start our own burrow," said another.

"Far away," added the third.

They decided to go away that same evening.

When Silla learned what they were planning, she protested. "What do you think you are doing, going away from home? Who knows what could happen to you!"

But her children argued, "We'll be very careful. It's all right, we can take care of ourselves."

"We've brought them all up to know what they need to know," offered Rahm. "We must let them make their own decisions now. Besides—" he looked tenderly at Silla—"there will be new children to look after before too long."

"That may be, but it is still difficult for me," said Silla. "These were my first."

Rahm had begun to wash his ears. Silla looked out across the meadow where her grown-up children had disappeared into the dusk.

She sniffed, listened, and crouched in the grass. And while she nibbled on a soft, sweet blade, she thought with resolve, *The moon will soon be full, and the cabbage heads will be round. Everything happens as it should—in its own time.*

TILDE MICHELS is one of Germany's favorite authors for children. Born in Frankfurt, she has lived in France and England and currently resides in Munich.

KÄTHI BHEND has won numerous awards for her books, including the 1982 Zurich Children's Book Prize and the 1986 Vienna Children's Book Prize for the Swiss edition of *Bad Times for Ghosts*. She lives in the canton of Appenzell, Switzerland.